About the Author

"Hello"

My sincere apologies as I really don't know how to give an author's introduction. This is my first book and I am very excited  *to know about your review. Please write back to me the review about the book to successgrooming@gmail.com. I promise I'll give a better introduction about myself in my next book.*

For You From Me!

Evincepub Publishing

SMIG - 65, Parijat Extension, Bilaspur, Chhattisgarh 495001

First Published by Evincepub Publishing 2017
Copyright © Shashank Nandakishor 2017
All Rights Reserved.
ISBN: 978-1-5457-1056-2

For you From Me

Shashank Nandakishor

<u>*Thank You*</u>

To all my teachers, mentors, guides and the entire JGI Family.

To my parents and my Family .

To all my Friends.

To Mr. Raghavan Iyengar, for the book cover design.

To Ms. Meghana Manjunath, for helping me in editing the content of the book.

About the book

Thank you reader! for choosing 'For you.. From me!'

For you, from me!

This is a book For you, from me!

Whenever someone is gifting something to someone, we do mention for whom it is and from whom it is. This is a story of a person who is willing to gift the rest of his life to the love of his life.

This book is dedicated to all the true lovers who expressed their love, who are about to express their love, who are still hiding their love and also to those who are at the other end of the above situations!

-Shashank Nandakishor

Prologue

For you, from me!

There are numerous answers to the one question called Love. Love is as simple as to understand a person. Isn't it?

The story starts from a guy who is attracted by a beautiful girl, if that is what is called crush at first sight, and then it is. How a crush and attraction can turn into love is the best part of the story!

It is actually the story most people can relate to. It is a compulsory experience in a lifetime of every individual existing with a heart.

That feels before expressing love to your loved ones is the most nervous moment in anyone's life. It is not so easy to expect one sided answers, if it goes the other way around, you shall hurt yourself without anyone's help! It's nobody other than you who has the capability of hurting you the most! And yes, the other way around, happiness cannot be expressed! And Love is the best part of every life! But love is not life. And there is life after love.

———— ◦ ————

Note:

Any character or the story in the book resembling to any individual, living or dead is completely fiction and imaginary creativity of the author.

Smoking and drinking is injurious to health.

For You From Me!

You don't know,

How many times I've typed the same text back and forth.

You don't know,

How many times I've deleted a text back and forth.

You don't know, how much you mean to me!

You don't know how much I want you to be with me.

You don't know,

How hard it is to imagine life without YOU!

I am not afraid in telling you what I feel about you,

I am afraid to listen to the reply from you.

I know I'm gonna be hurt, but it's important you to be not.

You are so much more important to me than you think,

When I'm with you, my eves don't even blink.

I look at you like a child, because you are one,

The innocence, the weirdness can compete none.

I don't love you because of your looks,

I love you, because it's you!

Let's get started!

The First time I saw her, was during my internship days in College. Yeah, I chose not to go out as my college has been my home since my PUC, B.com and now masters. She had come for a dance practice after college hours. Of the hundred and odd people, she was the one who grabbed my attention.

I don't think it was because she was dancing the best, I think it was because she was trying to match dance steps looking at others like the cute kindergarten kid. I was watching her dance from the fifth floor, a couple of floors above from where she was dancing. She was wearing a blue T-shirt. She looked like a child dancing, because when kids dance, they really don't care who is watching them, nor they don't care what people think of what they are doing. It was kind of similar to that, very cute indeed! Those moments are still right in front of my eyes, which I shall never forget. Even today after so many years. Her eyes have a magical magnet of attracting. She doesn't attract by her looks, she attracts by her cuteness and childlessness.

The second time I saw her, she looked like a lost angle in white, waiting for someone in the fifth floor. If I have had my wish powers, I would have wished that someone she was waiting should have been me!

She was there, standing alone for almost ten minutes, and I almost walked three-four times close to her, figuring how to start up a conversation. That's when the boys think weird stuff and completely make fool of themselves.

What's the time? I thought of asking. My watch looked pretty attractive which she would have noticed and I also had a phone in hand, if I had asked her for time, it would have made me look a decent idiot!

I later thanked the college's last bell of the day, for helping me control my eagerness as her friends joined her. She was lost in between them. My heart felt low for not having to have a word with her.

The third time I saw her was when I had invited her for an event in college. Yes, I had invited her. Yes, by then we had already started talking! Thanks to facebook and her interest in knowing about a short movie audition that was going on in college.

I don't think she knew, but I was waiting for her, I was waiting to meet her for the first time. If she does remember I was at the entrance of the college's seminar hall to welcome her. I sent her in and I followed her after a couple of minutes, just to pretend I was busy. I find a seat next to her. Oh my God! I was sitting next to her, whispered my heart. She did look much prettier than in photos on facebook and instagram, could notice that based on my research.

Was I in love with her already? Or was it just infatuation? I did not bother much because spending time with her was more important than wasting time thinking about something else which didn't matter back then.

Though it was a Kannada event, being a die heart kannadiga, I was more interested in having small conversations with her. By then I had almost known her pretty well. Since the day we started to chat, our phones have seen each other's texts every single day. There hasn't been a single day of silence between us. Forget single day, I don't think there is even half a day of silence till now.

There are times, a lot of times, I wish for these days between us without silence lasts forever!

She sent me a forty seconds song recording in her voice, there hasn't been a single day yet that I have slept without listening to it at least five times! Not because she is a great singer, it's because the song was sung by her. Even now, every time I listen to it, I fall in love with her voice over and over again.

February 13th it was, she usually goes off at the night before eleven. But that day I had asked her to stay awake till midnight. I didn't let her sleep, though she wanted to. I wanted to give her a small surprise on what they call it as the Valentine's Day! She asked me a several times what surprise was it, and I never revealed until mid night. I hope she liked the pencil sketch I had made of her. I have done a lot of these, but hers was the first one I got it right in the first try! She said that was the first sketch anyone ever drew of her. I said I will be a lot of firsts in her life. I had only sent a picture if it though. I framed it and handed it over to her a month later in the college parking. She said she will go home and open it. I insisted her to make a video, so that I could see her expression.

Two minutes she couldn't resist. She opened it in in the parking only. She was happy, which made me happy.

She once told me to show that sketch to my wife after I got married, and I asked her to stand in front of mirror and hold the art facing mirror after marriage. I used to have a lot of such flirty talks with her. I loved irritating her; she would look even cuter when she got mad. I felt proud being reason for her being mad. Not just because she gets mad, it was because I could sense she was smiling even if she gets mad at me!

There was one time when I asked about her Dad, and her reply was something I did not know how to react. I was so sorry for bringing it up. I couldn't see her tears, but I could sense how much she loved him, and how badly she misses him!

'For all I can say, he should always be the second half of your name. And he is always with you, in your success. His blessings are there which results in the hard work you put in and in your achievement.' I said her.

'I am the bravest girl', she came back smiling though I could know the presence of her tears rolling on her cheeks.

She indeed is the bravest kiddo!

I like to call her Childu, and I always will, even when our hair turns grey! I will call her Childu. The child in her is always active; in fact, she is the child who is always active.

Coming back to the Kannada event we were sitting together in. I get a call in between and I had to go out, when I came back, my heart kind of broke as she was sitting with unknown people and there was no seat near her for me. I felt so sorry for making her sit alone! I did call her as I found a couple of seats in the front; she couldn't hear me as the audio in the event was loud. I still hope she had a good time that day, which was an unforgettable day for me. The most memorable day, as that was the day I spoke to her for the first time face to face.

After the event, I walk down with her till basement 1, where her dio was parked, and we took our first selfie picture. This is my best memory of all time until then!

All I did that day was waiting for her until she came and miss her after she left.

There is a reason why we meet a few people in life. She turned out to be the most special person I ever could have met.

All the time while we were walking together till basement, there was only one thing going on in my head! I told her about my thought to her the same evening. That was to ask her to go out for some coffee! A lot can happen over a cup of coffee! That didn't happen, I told her the reason for not asking as well, and that I was afraid that if she had given me a negative reply, I would have that fear or a negative thought while asking her out next time!

But she said she would have come if I had asked! I do regret that still! All the time we have spent together would have increased by a couple of hours!

Your brain is actually more active when you are talking to your crush. By the time you figure out a question you want to ask, the complete described analysis of possible answers and what next would have already been calculated in your head.

She has a lot of followers, in terms of guys behind her and guys who had proposed her in the past. I didn't know if she was seeing someone or not. I did ask her, more than a couple of times, apparently; also I did tease her with a guy who liked her. It was not because I wanted to tease her, but just to make sure she wasn't going out with anyone, and I didn't want to get in between anything complicated to make it even more complicated!

No wonder she has such a huge list of followers, with such beautiful adorably cute looks, who doesn't want to fall in for her. I do wonder how many more are still out there not able to express!

I do consider it is my luck that she was not interested in a relationship, because if she was, she would have been with someone before I even got to know her!

The second time we met! It was the most special day for me in terms of my profession. I had just started a company; I was in a training and taking motivation sessions for undergraduate students in our college. That day, I actually got to take a session for a post graduation class, which was also featured on the University website of the college.

As soon as I came out of the class, I heard my phone ringing, and after knowing it is her, my heart started to ring. She was in college. We spoke for a while and she had cold badam milk while I had boost in the college canteen. We together walked down to parking near her dio was parked and she dropped me near the entrance and left.

I couldn't have asked for a better day. I could spend a lifetime looking into her eyes. In her orange top, her presence with me, I could sense her presence with me like the presence of the sun in the sky. Can you hide sun on the brightest summer mid day? Try it without any shades on.

Her cuteness can match none; even small kids feel jealous looking at her childishness. The word queen was probably named after her.

She gave me a book, Chetan Bhagath's "half girlfriend". That was the first book I ever read. I had earlier tried to read books; I would successfully stop reading within ten to fifteen pages. I am so guessing she gave me this book and said that it's her favorite, defiantly had something to motivate me to complete it. And interestingly, the couple in the book also reads Chetan Bhagath's books!

Before I even realize, I had completely fallen in love with her. She meant more important to me than anything else in the world.

My eyes were busy looking for her everywhere; poor eyes didn't know she was always present in my heart.

The day she gave me the book! Actually, she had preparatory exams going on. She said she would give me the book on the first day of her exams, but she didn't because of her busy schedule after the exam. And on the second exam it was her friend's birthday and she went out to celebrate. I would be totally lying if I said I wasn't expecting to meet her or if I said I scheduled my time table to make sure I had time to meet her. And the third exam I suppose, I had least expected to meet her, I was sitting in my class after a long time.

Oh yes, I am a post graduate student in the same college she is pursuing b.com. My phone rang, I was so happy to see her name! I didn't even answer, before answering I took permission from the faculty before the call ended that I would return in fifteen minutes as I had to do a class presentation for my internal marks. As soon as I picked up the call she said she is in the third floor with the book. Was I interested in reading the book?, I asked myself.

I ran down from the sixth floor to the third floor in a fraction of seconds, and when I saw her inside the staff room, I waited outside. I was actually watching her and waiting for her, but as she came out I pretended like I was busy with my phone. She had the book which she handed over to me; I thought of skipping the class presentation and ask her out for lunch. But my friends kept calling me as it was our turn next!

I should thank that teacher for whom she was waiting to submit her assignment, as she was still waiting 'as I went up finished up my presentation as quick as I could and came back!

There was a PG fest going on, we had to shout to talk. Even with all the noise around, I could still hear my heart beat which is till beating only for her!

I was still afraid to ask her to go out somewhere, probably for lunch. I asked if she have had lunch. She said "no". I took a deep breath and asked, "We'll go out for lunch then?"

I think I left her with no choice as she was hungry too. She said it was a very intelligent way to ask out.

"Biryani", I said. Something that she couldn't say no again! I knew her pretty well by then. We ordered two chicken Biryani, a chicken side and two sprites. That was the longest time I took to finish a Biryani, as I was not just eating. I love those tiny little conversations we have. Especially, when I prank referring her as my girlfriend or wife. I do that all the time, she gives a weird expression which is between shy and anger! Can there be an expression as such? Am I creating new expressions?

She actually finished an entire Biryani! She is indeed my kind of girl, I said to myself! By the way, Biryani is always my first love.

We did meet a lot after that; in fact, we met every time she came to college. She hardly comes, as she was doing another course apart from B.Com outside college and has permission to skip B.Com classes to attend those other classes. That one day where we sat in the fourth floor corridor for almost two hours. There are so many people who have complimented the dimple on my cheek, but her compliment on that day was worth having a dimple.

We spoke a lot that day. She used to talk about how she avoids when guys flirt with her. She said if anyone irritates her, she would reply, 'Ok bro, chill'. That 'bro' would have broken a guy's heart like a billion times at once!

There could have been none who has flirted and irritated her as much as I have. I was not being in that 'bro' list, it made me feel so special. Beware! Girls use 'bro' as a weapon of heart destruction!

She made me sit in the library, actually she didn't. But I went along with her. So that I could be with her for some more time. One hour, that was the longest duration I ever stayed in the library! I spent the entire time looking at her and exactly doing what she didn't want me to do, disturbing her! She looks pretty when she pretends to look mad at me.

Two warnings did come from the librarian, indicating me to look at the 'silent please' sign board. I did see and said the librarian that I would defiantly try to. But how could I, we belong to a generation where we don't listen to anyone and especially in India; sign boards have no value at all.

That period of time when you are in love and before expressing it, there is actually no explanation for that feeling! One who experiences will only know that exact feel. Some feelings have no explanations! It's like happiness and sadness along with another friend called confusion mixed thoroughly.

Once she did ask, "Dude, do you seriously like me or just playing around?", while we were sitting in the library! I could hear my heart beats, and feel my blood move like a huge breeze in the ocean and breathing in and out with eyes almost popping out. I was freaked out and didn't respond. I actually did not know what to respond. Should I have had said yes? Should I say have had said no? Or was it the best for me to remain silent?

And many more questions started playing who is gonna answer who! I somehow realized that I have not uttered a word for a long time now and that I should say something. I still didn't know what to say and then I again realize she was waiting for an answer from me! My lips just moved, I still didn't know what would have said if she hadn't stopped interrupting me. She came back saying, "You call me Childu right? See how tough questions I can punch".

That punch hit right in my heart, which was already lost in her eyes.

That was a good one, only girls know how to put boys in trouble. As she said that I started thinking from another angle.

If I tell her the truth and if her reply would positive, there would have been no problem. But if she had a negative reply, I would lose not only the hope of spending the rest of my life with her, but also lose the most special friend I have ever met.

Once a relationship is lost, you can never get it back! That's the one reason I'm still afraid of. I don't even want to dream about losing my Childu!

I did want to know what she was thinking, but I had no guts to fire a question related to it. This is again the exact kind of feeling that cannot be expressed I, was earlier talking about.

How can I even imagine losing her even when my dreams are filled with her smiles!

Talking about dreams! I have most of the times said this to her just before wishing good night. "Okay bye.. We shall continue talking in dreams!" She always and still laughs when I say this. And the next day I would also ask, "did I come in your dreams?' I wonder will I ever get a positive reply from her for that someday!

I did once actually have had a dream and I also told her about it, for which she replied 'awww'. We are old and hypothetically keeping hundred as lifespan. As I am three years older to her, she asks me, "Dude, you'll die three years early right? Won't I get bored for three years?" and my reply should be given the best dialogue award, "chill Childu, our great grandchild will keep you engaged until we meet again upstairs!" "Awww, that is so sweet", she replied.

That was not just a dream I had during night, it was also something I started day dreaming thereafter! 'Am I thinking too much about her?' Said my mind. 'Do I have anything more important than her to think about?' heart softly replied.

There are usually only three activities she does in her daily life, 'Eat, sleep and read', texting me has slowly added on to the list. And her mood swings faster that tide! One minute she is happy and looks annoyed the very next minute. She is like a kid who gets irritated and cries when a kid doesn't get sufficient food or sleep!

I think I'm already used to her mood swings; I can sense her mood and react accordingly. Even her anger looks damn cute. If there was any all time cute tournament, this Childu would have won without any competition, considering even small kids could compete!

Tradition and culture in her is something hard to find in girls of today's generation. If that is in her, it is only because of how her mom has lifted her! Her mom is her real hero!

Raising a single daughter is no easy task!

Most of the times, we both do think and act similarly. Our tastes and preferences are together. Caste/Religion everything is the same, which will avoid any of the family problems arising in future. I have thought a lot, about us. About her and me being together forever. She is a princess, she should and always be one. I am not boosting myself by calling me a prince, I may or may not be, but she is my beautiful princess!

I have thought a lot, about us. About her and me being together forever. She is a princess; she should and always be one. I am not boosting myself by calling me a prince, I may or may not be, but she is my beautiful princess!

Whenever I do think of her, without even my notice there is a smile in my face, and after a while I figure out that I am awkwardly staring something or someone and just smiling!

I wish we were friends right from the birth! Nineteen years since she was born we hadn't met. We meet everyone at the right time for the right reason. After I met her, she has been the reason I smile!

March 28th, 11:56 PM. I can never forget the time and date. That was the time, when I proposed love to the love of my life. Since then until the next day evening, I had been in a complete shock. Did I actually do it? That was actually something she asked as well, "Did you just say that?", she also asked if I was serious or just playing around.

I think she already knew by then, but I am not sure that she knew. "I love you more than anybody can ever love a person!", those were the exact words I said.

That moment felt like she said yes, I felt like I was on top of the world. All I could think about was to never let her down and to always be with her, being a reason for her happiness!

I did know that she was going through a lot of complications already in her life. I did not wish to tell this to her and disturb her exam preparations. CA is not an easy task. Her exams were a couple of months later. I was carried away by the moment and happen to express what I felt towards her.

But she does not know that there are no complications when involved with me!

She might have seen love as a burden and an added responsibility, but she doesn't know love is a gift of life and I was there to support her not to distract her!

I never knew she would look at me as a complication!

"What did I do?", I asked myself. Yes, I was willing to gift my life to her by promising to spend the rest of my life with her. That moment when I did tell her that I could feel her excitement, I could sense her acceptance, I could be ready to accept her as my responsibility. She wasn't feeling well when I proposed to her. She did want me to talk to her and so I was. I had written a poem. Obviously, for her, but I just showed her and asked how is it. After reading she took it a little serious and asked, "did you write this for me?, think and answer I won't ask again", she said. I said yes. And I didn't let her talk much as she wasn't feeling well. I said we will talk tomorrow. She said "ya tomorrow", and signed off!

I couldn't sleep the entire night. All I thought was about her and our future and how amazing it would be to spend life together forever. I also had thought about how to introduce her to my parents!

Is love only about sharing the rest of your life with a person? Or is it important that the other person being happy with or without you? When you don't get something there are a lot of unanswerable questions that your brain asks you!

There is a lot of difference when you ask your brain a question and when your brain asks you a question!

When you ask a question to your brain, brain is capable of thinking and answering, as it is its job to do so! But when brain asks a question, it expects heart to think and answer! Heart always wants to get involved in everything! Why can't it just pump blood and not interfere in anything else! Life would have been much better. And with heart *doing a lot of thinking, results in disaster answers! Follow your heart, but do carry your brain along!*

I did not talk to her for a few days. All I could think about was her and me and our future together. And that was all I had spoken to her in the last couple of days. I knew she was annoyed and irritated, but she didn't react much. Like a baby, as I said before, when kids don't get enough food or sleep, they cry.

I didn't know what to do. I couldn't stay for long without talking to her. She is a friend. I was thinking wheather to talk or not. Or rather I was thinking what to talk. One week passed by.

She didn't call or text either. My brain this time became a villain. It started giving in a lot of wrong inputs. She and I would be in constant touch through call or texts every single time and constantly know what each other was up to doing.

'Isn't she missing me?', 'Am I a fool who is completely lost in her by missing her?', 'Don't she have a little courtesy to ask how was I doing?'. A lot of questions. Before I figure out was it brain or heart questioning, my phone beeps.

It was her. She sent me a message after eight days. It reads, 'Miss you... Got to talk.' I typed a huge paragraph. I deleted it all and called her. She said hello, I heard a sweet voice after eight days, which I felt like eight decades. Before I even revert back, she asked "can we meet? I need to talk to you". "I will pick you up in twenty minutes", I said. She said she would come by herself to the coffee shop nearby college in 20 minutes. You know girls, their 20 minutes means 40 minutes. I reached the coffee shop in 30 minutes.

Surprisingly, she was there! 'How could she be on time?', I wondered. I could sense that something is wrong or something is about to get wrong. There are only three reasons for girls to be on time. One, if she is studious and it is time for class. Two, if she wants something or three, if she is meeting someone special. I was trying to be a lecturer in college, but I don't think she expected me to take class, so I was wondering if she wanted something or was I special to her. I walked towards her. She gives me a casual hug as usual. She ordered a strawberry milkshake and I ordered a cappuccino. The waiter asks me, "What sir long break? Not to be seen these days". "Yeah, I was busy with work", I said.

Oh, did I not mention? **I had life before I met this girl.**

I had just joined b.com, a lot of my puc classmates were my classmates again. Samartha, Ruthuparna, Raghunandan, Vishal and me. We were five inseparables. Samartha was from Tiptur, a typical village guy, but the way he transformed himself was unbelievable. Right from the village slang language to his dressing style. He had a crush on a girl, whose first name started from P and second name from G, he used to exited every time he saw the board or a sticker reading 'PG for men'. Raghu was a little shy for those who didn't know him and a silent killer for those who knew. Mr. Ruthuparna is a special character who is always found in the lost and found department in the college. He once lost his bike and reacted like as if he lost a pencil! Vishal was new to our gang. We were all sitting in class except Ruthu; he would always be late for first class. He called me to check if I was in class or out. I had forgotten to keep my phone in silent. As I came to class a little late, all the back benches were occupied so I had to sit in first bench. My phone rang and my sir was standing tight in front of me. He asked me for my phone to confiscate; I had no choice but to give. As soon as the call gets cut, idiot Ruthu calls back again. Sir looks at the name and answers the call. Without even listening to 'hello' and recognizing the voice he says, "Shut up and come to the canteen as soon as class gets over".

Sir face looked strange, me and Samartha were wondering what might have happen. Sir asked, "Do you know whom you are talking to?" in the most polite voice. He is so idiot that he still didn't realize and said, "I know very well, you shut up and come fast!"

Sir hit the red button in my phone and asked me to get Ruthu along if I wanted my phone back. I went with him to staffroom where all teachers already knew us very well. It doesn't matter whom teachers notice or not, but the last bench students are very well noticed. We were in the second semester and by then all the teachers were waiting to take revenge on us for all the best behavior in class we showed. After following sir, for the rest of the day, I finally got my phone. We go to a bakery behind college where we usually hangout and we lit up a cigarettes. I was very angry on Ruthu and was starring him angrily! He tries to tell a joke and cool me down. He said, "I knew it was sir, I still said that because I couldn't have said that to him directly". Yes, it did cool me down a little after I give him a bang on his back. I wonder why most of the time we meet only weird, strange and also most loveable people as friends. Life without friends is like missing the letter 'f' from life, life becomes a lie without friends!

Our class was one of the most irritating classes to our teachers. Though they did love us, they hated us. Quite hard to explain that. Only back benchers will understand that feeling!

We students hate whatever teachers tell, but one day we will all realize why they used to tell us what made us hate them back then.

All my teachers are even today the best people in my life. Try this, just talk to one of your old teacher whom you haven't spoken to in a long time, and tell them what you are currently doing.

Happiness is defined there. Teachers don't expect anything more than a student's success.

Some teachers teach lessons from books, but many of them teach lessons to lead life. I still apologies to my teachers for all my mischievousness in class. They revert back telling, 'back then we hated those, but today we remember only those. We do not remember who scored distinction. But we do remember students like you'. I don't know if it was told sarcastic or not, but it was so damn true!

The waiter's interruption took me to my past. But here I was with this beautiful girl in the coffee shop.

It was after eight days she had decided to talk to me. I thought she was waiting for her strawberry milkshake to start conversation. I was already done with half cappuccino and her milk shake was half done too.

'My first thought in the morning is you, and my last thought in the night is you. I hear your voice all the time talking to me. I love you. I will love you for the rest of my life', I thought of telling those exact words and break the silence. But instead I lit up a cigarette, "since when did you start smoking again?" she finally spoke. "Just one here and there", I said inhaling smoke. "You know I don't like you smoking", she said holding her hand near her nose. "You know it well that I could not stand silence between us, and you didn't talk to me for eight days!" I shouldn't have said that. Silence extended for another five minutes, which felt like hours.

It was evening, twenty minutes to six. I took the last drag of the cigarette and lit it off in the ash tray. "How was your day?" she asked. "Just like the last eight days, all I did was to think about you". I replied leaning forward. She didn't move her lips. "How are you? How is everything going on?", I asked after sensing that she was feeling uncomforted. "I have thought about us, it just doesn't work out", she said in a very soft voice of hers.

Was that what I asked, I thought to myself. I did not know what to tell! She did not reply to what I asked. I too thought of telling something irreverent to what she said. I didn't realize all the while I was thinking about this, it was two minutes of silence.

I think silence was a bit long, she came back telling, "You are a nice person dude, and I don't have any reason as such to go against your thoughts. But then I have my own responsibilities and constraints, and it's too deep!" I still didn't know what to tell her or how to react.

On the other hand I didn't want to disturb her. Love is not something you can force on someone. In her absence my eyes would look for her all over, but poor eyes didn't know that her presence is in my heart! 'She will be there forever', said my heart. My mind also said, 'she will be in here too'. This is the first time ever that heart and mind have got a similar answer! And that's when tears roll down from your eyes!

She was looking right at me. I didn't want to show her my pain and confuse her further more.

I asked her, "Promise me, that this doesn't change anything. You will not act weird. And you will not stop talking to me!". "Why will I stop talking to you? You are the best and the sweetest friend I have", she said with a smile. I smiled looking at her smile, which made me forget about everything for a while. We decided to take off. She gave me a hug, a hug that felt like we were back being friends. "I will call you", she said before leaving.

I sat alone at the coffee shop after she left. I had half a pack of smokes, which by the end of my stay was all into ashes.

What am I gonna do? How am I gonna spend the rest of my life knowing she is not going to my love?

A series of unanswerable questions had only one answer in the form of her! She was everything to me from the day met her! The day I met her for the first time flashed in front of my eyes. If I already knew I would meet her, I don't think I would have ever fallen in love ever before I met her.

'Oh! Not again', I wasn't really going to think about my past. But unfortunately I had all sort of thinking going on!

The girls I went out with in the past are all happy. What else does a guy who truly loves want? Isn't it her happiness?

Yes, it is! But not with this girl. For whom I thought I would be the reason for her happiness. For whom I am willing to do anything to see her smile. Her smile has the power and ability to take away any problems. Her electrifying smile is more than sufficient to supply electricity to the entire world. Her smile is magic. Her smile is the most beautiful creation in this world. Oh! Wait, just like this! I was talking about something serious and I got carried away just by the thought of her smile.

I would get this strange thoughts one that doubt of her not being with me forever struck. She will have to end up with someone. It's okay if she is happy with him. But what if she is not! What if, the guy with whom she ends with is not as understanding and as caring as I am!

I am very sure that she will be happy with me! Why doesn't she understand that?

How can one expect the friendship which was there earlier to remain the same after proposing and things not working as you expected? I was so depressed for losing her friendship. It was almost eleven in the night and I was still in the coffee shop. I badly wanted to go have a couple of drinks. But I had quit drinking about more than a year and a half ago. I went home and couldn't sleep for the rest of the night.

I got a message from her, "I do understand what you said, but please understand from my point of view. I am really not ready for this now. Let's not talk about this hereafter. I don't want to lose a good friend like you. Good night". That message was worth having whatsapp in my phone.

She sent, 'please understand', I had earlier said her there would be no one as understanding as I would. "Good night", I reverted back and slept with a smile as she at least understood what I said to her and hoping for things to be normal from the next day. Is that possible? Yes and no, my heart and mind started.

Yes, it all seemed to be normal. Our talks were as usual as we used to talk before. We exchanged texts all the time. Things didn't change, and so the love and care I had for her in my eyes. Will she ever understand me? Or should I understand her? When we think similar in all the aspects, why not in this? Why not in deciding the future? Why do I only see her in my future?

This time it was not my heart or mind asking these questions. It was the tears trying to reach heart asking mind, where both of them had the same answer, 'I don't know!'.

There were a few incidents similar to this earlier when I fell in love during my undergraduate days. Samartha, I and Vishal were walking in the college corridor. We saw a girl. Like most of the times, when in a gang of friends are there and a really good looking girl passes by, everyone tends to fall in love at first sight in a fraction of a second. That's universal bachelor's fact. All three of us simultaneously said, "She is the one, she is your sister-in-law!", and then looked at each other's faces with weird looks.

While we followed her in the half way our beloved favorite lecturer caught us. "No other better work you guys have, go attend class?", he said. "Sir, we are outstanding students, we spend more time outside class than in class. We also go to class. But when there is no teacher inside", Samartha said. "Where are the other two idiots, Ruthuparna and Raghu", sir asked. "We forgot to tell them we are bunking, hence they are sincerely attending class", Vishal blabbered.

"You guys will never ever grow up", sir said while going to the staff room. We lost this beautiful looking girl in the meantime. We looked all over for her. "Excuse me", a voice from behind called us. We were least bothered to turn and revert back while we were still searching for her. "Can you please tell me where the staff room is?", a voice from behind asked. I turned back pointing at the staff room which was on the left side, third room from where we were standing. It was her! "Come even I am going there", I said and guided her through. The two idiots with me also came along.

"Here it is", I said. "Thank you", she said and went in. We waited outside for her to come, meanwhile looking at her from outside. "Ma'am my name is Meena, I wanted to check my internal marks", she said. "Meena", said all three of us together. Followed by the same weird look at each other again!

"Hey! Hi! Which year you are from?", I asked as she came out. "First year" she said with a smile. Our smile extended as we were her seniors. We were in second year. "How come we never saw such pretty beautiful girl in college before", Vishal started flirting. "That was because you were busy with your girlfriend!" said Samartha, striking off Vishal from the competition. Vishal was out of the scene. Samartha got a call, he cut it. He got a call again and went in search of Vishal. I later had to thank Vishal for creating a fake emergency and calling Samartha leaving me and Meena alone. "I figure you are the kind of girl who drinks coffee?" I asked. "Yeah, so?" she replied, seemed to be arrogant. "Just for information sake", I quickly replied. She laughed out loud telling, "look at your face!" "We'll go", she asked. "Why would I tell no? Shall we". She stopped by a small bakery nearby. "Here?" I asked her. She replied, "Why not? Don't you get coffee here?

I was shocked! Angels do exist, I felt! I was wondering should I smoke in her presence or not. By the time I thought of asking her if I could, she opened cigarettes from her bag and offered me one. "Do you?", she asked. First time I felt shy in telling yes. We had tea along with cigarettes. And that became mine and Meena's hangout place daily after college. She used to tell me about her ex-boyfriend, with whom she had broken up recently.

Meena was an open minded girl. She wouldn't think before talking. No matter what it is, she would tell it on face. Since the day we meet, we were almost together most of the times, apart from the classes she had to attend. Her class was a floor below mine, so that became our adda.

Me, Samartha, Vishal, Ruthu and Raghu were standing near her class. We had to go out as it was Samartha's birthday. We had to call Meena out of her class. We went near her class to check which teacher was inside, so that we could plan something to call her out.

Something we are used to doing a lot! Call out friends from class by making up fake stories. The door of her class was locked. Raghu pushed me so that the door was knocked. Everyone ran away. Luckily, it was our favorite sir. "This is not your class, this was your class in the last semester", said sir. "I know sir, I am here for Meena", I replied. Sir gave me a Nike arrow eyebrow look. I didn't know what reason to tell. Her classmates knew that she was close to me. They all started shouting 'oooooooh'. While she was busy shushing them all, sir asked, "Why do you want her?" I didn't know what to tell. Raghu from a distance where only I could see, was showing me thumbs up, asking if everything is fine. Thankfully, the bell rang to end the class. Sir went in to take attendance. All the idiots who pushed me and ran came back. Sir came out, "daily you people come to college, why aren't you guys seen in class?", that's what he asks us almost every time he meets us. "We sit in library and study sir", said Ruthu. "See you faces in mirror", sir said and walks away. "We do that daily", Vishal said. Sir didn't react.

Meena came out shouting, "can't you wait for five-ten minutes?", "I thought class doesn't get over for another hour", I replied. "See now, everyone got to know about us!", she said and walked in front. "Hey, stop!", I stopped her. "What is there between us?", I defiantly wanted an answer for that. Was eager to know what she was thinking. "Nothing is there, but everyone will now think that something is there", smartly she answered.

We went to a Samartha's flat, where he lived alone as his family was from a village and he studied here in the heart city and so called 'Garden City' of Karnataka. His flat was like a second home for all of us. We used to spend a lot of time there, a lot!

Meena was by then adjusted with going out with our all boys gang. The official cake cutting, cake eating and cake all over the face party was over. The sun was just about to be lost when we decided to leave. Meena and I had planned to go out, which we did not inform to any.

There is a reason for us to go out. In Samartha's place when everyone were busy talking and chatting about all possible non happening things, Meena and I were sort of having an eye to eye contest. It would have been a deep conversation at that point in time if we were alone. And when we got a chance to be alone, she whispered in my ears that she wanted to talk to me alone after later today. And that resulted in our coffee date.

She bravely took the initiative of starting the conversation, "morning near class you asked something remember?" A lot of things I asked, of that which was I supposed to remember, I wondered for a while. That's the problem with girls. They remember only what they want and expect us to remember the same. "Regarding?" I asked. "What is there between us?" At first I was tensed thinking it was a question fired at me. And then I realized that she just asked me to remember that little conversation we had near her class, and before I could relax, the tense moment was back *again. Oh my, are we gonna have this conversation now, I wondered. One thing I said to Meena, "Meena, no matter what, please do not apologise to me. I hate it when people do that as if I cannot understand them", "okay", she said.*

After I proposed to Childu we both had a little hesitating feel while talking to each other. A week later I and Childu had decided to catch up for lunch. Yes obviously, Biryani it was. One chicken Biryani and a coke each, we were full. Once done eating, we stop at a coffee shop for deserts.

One chocolate and cappuccino was our order. "How come you don't have cigarettes?" she asked. "My girlfriend doesn't like me smoking, so I quit", I joked. Joke was not about quitting, it was about the girlfriend. She got to know I was referring to her as my girlfriend. Just like old times. But it was not the same as before. It sounded funny to her before, but not funny anymore. "Ooh oh!", she said. I took a deep breath and smiled as she smiled and still took it in a lighter way. "Who is your girlfriend?" she acted like she seemed to be interested in knowing. I looked right into her eyes and said her that, "I'm right now looking right into her eyes". She leaned a little forward and my heart beat sounded like bullets sound. She went back laughing. And it felt like a bullet in my heart backfired!

Though everything was back to normal, I couldn't let go of one thing. Love! How can I spend the rest of my life, knowing she won't be in it!

She came in my life when I least expected her to come, and she left when I least expected her to leave.

She actually didn't leave completely. She only asked for permission to exit my heart. But she knew she could never be out of my life, as a friend.

Girls and saree, is the best combination ever. If guys had to compare it to, it would be cigarettes and tea.

It was graduation day for undergraduate students. It was the first time I would see her in saree. It was exact three years, since I had graduated from the same place. All my memories were re-cherished. Thanks to my heart for its continued interruption asking eyes to look for her.

She sent me a picture on whatsapp. It read, 'got ready, leaving for college now'.

I couldn't wait to meet Childu. I had asked her to call me as soon as she reached college. I wanted to meet her as soon as she came, and did not want to disturb her once she joins her friends.

In fifteen minutes she was here. I did not talk much as I met her, I could not! I was lost in the beauty of her sight. She looked simple and pretty, another deadly combination!

Orange saree, she wore. Of all the other graduate students, she was the only one I could see clearly. All the rest were blurred in the background.

How lucky is college? It witnesses all the memories, the friendships, the love, the fights, the breakups and so on. When we now tell that we miss college, it is not the actual college. It's all the above mentioned that we miss.

"You look pretty", I said looking in her eyes. "Thank you", she said. "I'll call you before leaving she said and joined her friends.

My job got confirmed in college after my post graduation in the same college. Yes, I wanted to work in the same college I studied. I got the job which I loved to do, training and interacting with students. The joy of working in the same institute I spent my entire college life was mind blowing. I still had to write a final exam of my post graduate course. I still had a month of student life in me.

I was waiting for her call. So that I could meet her again later that day while she was leaving. I was afraid that she would go out with her friends as it was their last memorable time in college.

Childu called me at 7:30. I had just been out for a smoke after waiting for almost two hours. She was waiting near my car in the parking lot.

"Didn't go out with friends?" I asked. "We'll go out for dinner?", she replied! Or rather was that a reply? I wondered. She does it all the time. If she doesn't want to answer a question she'll tell something that's not at all related.

How can I say no to Childu? It doesn't matter what she asks, when she asks or where she asks, I would never give her a negative reply.

Biryani again! The voice I love to listen to, the food I love to eat, the face my eyes love to see. Rain started to drizzle. Wasn't it the perfect evening?

"So, you were asking something?" she said. I hope referring to the conversation we had in the parking lot. "Why didn't you go out with your friends?" I asked. "You wanted me to go out with them? You tell yes, I'll go now also, yes is it?" in a flow she fired. "I was waiting for you only! Why would I not want you to come out with me?" "Hey, guess what?" I continued. "You are stupid, idiot, donkey, monkey..." she pretended to like guessing. "Stop, your guess may go on for a while". I stopped her. "Okay, tell what", she asked leaning forward. "Remember how badly I wanted to work in college? I got that job!"

She was fully shocked and surprised. She was so happy for me. "This calls for a definite celebration", she said.

"Yeah, let our exams get over, we'll celebrate", I said. We both had exams at the same time, a week's time we had from then for exams to start.

We were done eating. "You asked why I didn't go out with my friends, right?" she said as she took a tissue. "Yes", I replied. "Because if I had gone out with them, I couldn't have come out with you", she said. Did she just say that! She in saree, plus rain, plus dinner, plus she flirting? Oh my! It felt like the perfect time to ask her about reconsidering her thought about love.

"Why do you like me?" she asked. "I can't tell exactly why, but I haven't loved anyone as much as I love you. You are different. Your cuteness, your simplicity! Why shouldn't someone fall in love with you?" I said and I started wondering why she is asking this now! I continued, "Hey, I'm not telling that I cannot live without you! I will live. But I cannot definitely be happy without you". She looked in my eyes, she came a little closer. In a low voice she said, "Shall we leave?"

I said okay. And there was some awkward silence while we were walking till the car. "Why did you ask that?" I questioned her as we reached my car. She loves cars. She said she'll drive and sat in the driver seat. I handed over the keys to her. "You still didn't answer me?" I said. "You want me to answer your question or do you want to reach home safe?" she laughed after saying that. That wasn't funny enough for me to laugh. I held her hand and asked her, "Why?" "I don't know dude, I don't know why I asked, and I don't know what to do.", my heart beat increased. I couldn't let go of her hand. She didn't want me to either. I could feel that as she held on to it tight. "I will never let you be alone, I shall always be by your side", I said holding her hand even tight. "I need time", she said. I told her, "take as much as time you want, I know you will never take a bad decision. Whatever it is, let me know!" She started the car and we went back to college as her car was in college. She gave me a hug. This time it was a long hug. A tight hug too. 'No matter what happens, I don't want to lose you' or 'don't leave me forever". It meant either one of those.

She said, "Bye. Good night". "Good night, drive safe", I said and we both took off.

I did not see that coming. She had started to think about me? Consider me? I wish I could peep in her heart and mind to know what she was thinking about me!

Girls are very strange creatures; you can never even predict one percentage of what they might be thinking. By the time you get to know a little about what they are thinking, they would have started to think about something else you can't even imagine about.

"Reached home safe", she dropped in a text. I read and smiled. Before I could reply she sent another text, "I know that's what you would ask". "You can read my mind better than anyone", I replied blushing. I still don't know why, but I called her. She asked "what's up?" "I just wanted to listen to your beautiful voice", I said.

"All you did in the last three hours was that only know", she said. It was raining. Bangalore is the best place when it's raining. Three things that comes first in the minds of bangaloreans when it rains. Hot bajjis, coffee or tea and the person you love. The first two never even came into my mind, my heart overtook my mind. My heart is a place where there is place to none except her. Her voice in that romantic night was all I needed. I was lost in her voice. I was so lost that I didn't even listen to what she was telling. I could see water drops fall in slow motion. The smell of rain and talking to the person you love, how could I have resisted not saying the three magical words, I Love You!

I did whisper through my breath. She stopped, "sorry what?" I said, "Nothing", without even thinking. She asked me, "to think and answer". The first time she used this trump card, a lot happened. Though I love her to the extent which is beyond everything in my life, I didn't want to tell her then. Her happiness is all that matters, said my brain. Be reason for her happiness, bloody blood pumping machine always confused!

Love is a gift. This can be opened by two different set of keys! Those two keys are in the form of two different sets of eyes. The gift, love opens only when they meet!

Sometimes you meet someone, and it's so clear that the two of you, on some level belong together. As lovers, or as friends, or as family, or as something entirely different. You just work, whether you understand one another or you're in love. You meet such people once in a lifetime. Who will be the reason for you to believe in coincidences, or fate, or sheer blind luck? She was it! I always heard a voice in my head. I love you; I heard the voice in my heart every time I thought of her.

I always ask myself a simple question before doing something. 'A week, or a month, or a year from now, would I be glad for doing it?' Yes, was my first thought. Because I cannot even imagine even a fraction of a second without her.

There was only one thing in my list that would make me happy, and it was her, looking at her smile forever.

The time I spent with her was the most precious moments of my life. Ever since I tell her bye on the previous meet, I would desperately be waiting for a 'Hi' from her on the next meet. I couldn't wait for a day, from when she and I would never have to be apart. It was her, I would spend the rest of my life with, I always knew.

It was a Friday evening; I stood in front of God in a temple. My only wish was to be with her as long as possible. I finished my prayers, opened my eyes and turned towards my right. It was her! She was standing there, looking at me. I at first thought I was dreaming, but then she said 'hi' with her eyes. She had come to the same temple with her mom. With her mom standing beside her, she barely reacted. I could sense that it was the right time to play with her mixed reactions. When people visit the temple, they usually go round the temple odd number of times. Her mom did and she followed. I went right behind her. Nine rounds it was. Was a big temple indeed, but with her, walking was easy. Just like I imagined the rest of my life would be with her. That was the first time I saw her mom. It is true; most girls get their charming and beautiful looks from their moms.

People sit for a while before leaving the temple. I don't know the reason behind that, but heartily thanks to whoever started that. She was sitting alone while her mom went inside temple again with someone who just came.

"What's up?" I asked. "How come you've come to the temple? Since when religious and all?" as usual again, she questioned my question. "If I knew my prayers would be answered soon, I would come daily", I said. "What prayers dude", she asked and wrinkled. "I just prayed that I should spend the rest of my life with the love of my life and opened my eyes, she was the one I saw. Looking at me, her eyes filled with love". I replied, looking at her. She was looking at me in a different way. Two minutes passed, she didn't talk. "What happen Childu?" I asked. "Nothing, sir", she said. She continued, "I don't want to think dude, I'll leave all my life related decisions to my mom", she said half heartedly. "Childu, listen", I said softly. "What", she said with a tone dragging the 'a' in what. "Think once Childu, you don't have to think again, forever! I'll do all the thinking for you, for the rest of our life!"

Her mom came back before Childu could even think of answering for it. She introduced me as her senior in college. "Hello aunty", I said. Aunty was so sweet. She spoke to me as if she knew me well. While leaving aunty also said, come home sometime. "Sure", was the word that came out of my mouth. But my heart was insisting to tell, 'why sometimes, I'll come all the time'. They left, and so did I. Through hand signal she gestured telling she would call me later.

I went to a nearby bakery, lit up a smoke and ordered for a tea. 'There is a serious relationship talk today for sure'. My mind said. 'Don't worry, whatever happens, she is yours', heart consoled telling that to mind.

Is she getting confused and confusing me to? She knows how much I love her; she knows she is going to be happy for the rest of her life with me. What else is bothering her? Some answers I want, but I know she won't give them easily.

Childu, for once stop acting like Childu!

For the first time, I was afraid to answer her call. I didn't answer, not because I liked my ringtone, because I didn't know how to face her tone. "Hey, call back when you are free", she dropped in a text. What if it was something *important? I called her back as soon as this thought struck me.*

"Childu, tell me", I asked as she picked up the call. "I don't know what to tell you dude". She said in a very low voice. "What happen Childu", I took the same tone as hers. "I don't know. It's not that I don't like you or something, but at the same time I don't want to hurt my mom. And I also don't want to tell you something and keep up your hopes on me. I don't know dude, I am so confused". "Childu, don't take any decision in this confusion. It is about your life. Your one decision is gonna decide the rest of your life. Trust me; you won't be hurting your mom. If you are happy, even she will be happy, and you know it very well that you will be happy with me.

Don't tell anything now. Take your time, tell my whenever and whatever you feel like telling. I love you, and I will forever", I said her calmly.

I don't understand how I am able to give such good advices, I usually don't give any advices, and most of my advices are written off, as it will be a complete disaster.

When it comes to her, even the worst in me becomes the best. That's how much I love her. That's how much I want her to be with me. I made a promise to myself that night, whatever the situation is, I will take care of her and I will love her for the rest of my life, no matter what!

It was a Sunday afternoon, my phone started ringing and so did my heart as it was her call. "Hello", I said. She didn't talk. She was feeling low, her breath told me. I knew she wanted to meet. But I insisted as to I wanted to. "I'll come near the coffee shop near your place, will you join?" I asked. "Okay", she replied.

She came there with a dull face, I knew something was wrong. I didn't ask her anything. I started a conversation to divert her thought. "Hey..." she interrupted me there and said, "I miss my dad so much dude". She lost her dad a few years ago. I had hardly asked about her dad. Every time I asked, she would go off. I would always divert her when any related dad topic comes up when she is with me. I didn't know what to tell her. But I had to tell her something. If not, she would have started to weep. "Hey Childu, you are such a brave girl. You should not be sad like this. I am here! I know I cannot fill your dad's shoes. But I will try to", it seemed like that's what she wanted to hear as well. She did smile, a half hearted smile. Why all of a sudden you are thinking about all this?, I was about to ask. I was wondering if it was the right way to ask or not. I wanted to make sure it wouldn't hurt her. It hurts me more to see her being hurt. Before even I was about to ask, she replied.

"I was filling up a form for higher studies abroad, and there was a section asking 'Father's name and occupation' dude, I could not fill it. I felt like crying. So I only called you". "Don't worry dude, I am there for you, and I will be there for you no matter what", I said consoling her.

But, wait! What? Higher studies in abroad? "What higher studies? didn't You tell about that till now?" I asked Childu. "Ya dude, one year course, I'm thinking to study abroad", she replied. It was still not confirmed, but I already started thinking was that necessary! One year, she and I, in different countries! Anyway, I knew that wouldn't happen, as she was the only daughter and her mom wouldn't have sent her. More that I missing her, her mom would miss her the most. And that topic never even came up again.

Rain! It started to rain!

"We'll go", she stood up. "Are you crazy? See how heavily it's raining. You'll catch up cold. Shut up and sit", I said as she looked angrily at me. I smiled and she was still looking at me. I laughed. She forgot why she came to meet me, she had completely forgotten about why she was sad and she looked so happy, that is what I had promised myself that I would give her. "What", she asked adding a lot if a's in between what! "Let's go", I said. We ran towards my car in the heavy rain. "I don't want to go in car", she cried like a kid. Her home was a couple of roads away. I took a jacket from the car to give it to her. "Don't get so filmy, I won't fall for all this", she said and started to walk. I put the jacket back and walked fast towards her. Half way down, we stood near a tree, she started rubbing her hands. "That's why I gave you jacket, not for the filmy feel", I said. "Go home and drink hot water or milk", I said. "Okay sir", she said and paused. "You only buy me milk, hot, now!" she ordered.

I looked around, and found a small tea shop. "It's so hot dude", she said. "It's hot because it's in your hand and so are you", I replied as she shied away. She was holding the coffee class in both the hands. I stretched my hands and hold hers. She looked into my eyes, tears almost rolled out of my eyes. That was the happiest moment till date in my life. 'Childu, I love you', I wanted to say. But my voice and those words got stuck in my throat. "You want to tell something?" she asked. "No, but I want to hear something", I said, holding her hands even tight. She took a sip of coffee and looked into my eyes. I too took a sip from the same cup. "Even I want to hear, why I should tell. Go", she said in the most cutest and childish way. "Okay I'll go leave", I said and turned and took a step forward and stopped in shock! "Hey stop", Childu said, though I had stopped. I stopped and blanked out, when I said I'll go to Childu and turned back, it was Meena. Standing right in front of me! I and Meena were standing facing each other and looking at each other. I didn't know how to react.

Childu came in between forming a triangle and saw both of us looking at each other.

Meena had come out to buy some groceries, could make that out, looking at the cover and items visible inside that. She didn't talk anything; she just walked away past us. I turned back as she went past us, and after she passed, I looked at Childu, who was wondering who she is and why this silence was.

"Who is she?" Childu asked. "She was my junior in college. And a best friend", I said and continued the story from where I'd stopped.

Meena and I were sitting in the coffee shop, sipping coffee. Where she started the conversation about where our friendship was going. I took a deep breath and said, "Meena, if you tell yes, I will spend the rest of my life with you". After telling that, I was preparing for a long speech in my mind. "Yes", she said. I didn't realize, what I asked, completely baffled. "You said you want to spend the rest of your life with me, if I said yes. And yes I said". I was speechless, though I had prepared for whole another speech.

I was so happy that I could barely remember the rest of the evening in the hangover of love. But yes, I do remember we did spend almost an hour walking in the road after that.

Every day and every time we met, I love you and I love you too was something that we spontaneously got used to. By the time we realized that we were spending a lot of time in getting to know about each other, a couple of weeks passed by in a flash. My friends started complaining that I'm not spending much time with them and I'm completely into her all the time. Yes, I was completely into her, I didn't realize that until one day when she said she is taking her mom to the hospital and I caught her going on a bike with a guy. My friends were with me. They said me "it's okay, don't worry. We are with you". I still had the possessiveness, as I said it might have been her brother.

The next day we met, "How is your mom? What had happened?" I asked. "She is fine. Just a general check-up", she replied. "I saw you Meena. I saw you with a guy". I said.

I would have blindly believed if she had said that she was her brother or cousin. Come on man, she was the women I loved. That trust should obviously be there. "Sorry", she said. I didn't even want to listen to her explanations. I just left from there. She called my name a couple of times, and I heard it. I didn't give a damn about it.

Coming back to Childu, "I still didn't hear to her explanations. She called me a lot, I didn't answer even for once. I blocked her on all social media and made sure she couldn't reach me", I said. Childu looked at me in silence. "You would have done the right thing obviously leave", she said.

"Didn't you ever feel like falling in love with anyone?" I asked. "Yes dude, I have felt like, but you know the families. Can't take any risk". "Hey, if you are happy obviously your mom will be happy", I said. "Ya, I know. I don't know what to do", she said in confusion. I explained her how our life would be in future.

I said what all I had in plan for her. She listened to all very excited. That's something I didn't make it up at that point in time. That was something I had planned for our future. I wanted to spend every single minute of my life with her. She is my dream. She is my princess. I had every single plan for a lifetime of happiness with her and I told her everything. "Dude, don't keep so much hope on me", she said. I was happy, my heart flew high as she didn't tell me to completely let go of hope. She said 'don't keep so much hope', that doesn't mean to she said to stop dreaming and kill all my hopes. She asked, "I am standing between sea; tell me how to come to the shore. I don't know what to do. You tell me what can I do? I don't want to hurt my mom". "Childu, I will swim where ever you are, I will come along with you to the shore", I said. "Hmm we'll see", she replied.

We left. I dropped her back near her home. "Don't be like that, it won't suit you. Be smiling, everything happens for a reason", she said, looking at my face ever since I saw Meena. I did smile, in fact a smile with a big relief.

"Yes, everything happens for a reason. If I had still been committed to her, I wouldn't have met you and been this close to you", I said. She laughed and said bye. She walked near the gate and said the same as I smiled and took off.

Meena taught me how to love, but Childu showed me what love is.

I thought of proposing her officially in the most romantic way possible. I had planned everything. To take her out for a candle light dinner, go for a long ride. It was rainy season and it would have obviously rained. I had planned to make some excuse as my car broke and get down in the rain. She likes to get drenched in the rain; she would have obviously gotten down. Once she got down, I wanted to get down on one knee and tell her those three magical words.

Two days later, I was in college, working in my office. I received a text from her. 'I think I'm going to get into a relationship'. I bounced in happiness. 'I am waiting', I replied in the outmost excitement of my life. 'I am going to get committed to a classmate of mine. Still waiting?' She replied.

Within five seconds, the outmost excitement and happiness of my life, turned completely opposite. I texted her twice, asking if she was *kidding.* "*She replied,* "*I am serious, don't keep asking the same. Talk to you later, bye*", *I couldn't control the emoting rolling down in my eyes.*

I took permission from my boss and went to washroom and locked myself for a while. I went to terrace and sat there for almost a couple of hours without even realizing the time and only hoping that she was kidding. My heart became as heavy as it could. Water continuously rolled down from my eyes. I could not explain my situation. I dialed her number a few times and finally called her.

"What happen? Do you know what did you just say?" I questioned. "Yes, I finally know what I am doing", she replied. "Who is he?" I asked her, wiping tears from my eyes. "I will tell you soon once are sorted out", she replied. I then asked her, "how far is this reached?", "80% loading", she replied. "I am happy for you", I said and cut the call. But I was defiantly not happy. She meant more than anybody else to me. I could understand what is she willing to tell or thinking just by looking at the way her texts or just by listening to her voice.

As much as I was depressed, I was also afraid. Yes, I was afraid. If by any chance something goes wrong, I am very sure she won't be able to bear the pain of being hurt. She is a cute princess, who should always be smiling. On one hand, I was happy for her as she found someone she is happily willing to spend her rest of her life is. And on the other side, it's exact opposite emotion as that someone who isn't me!

It was one of such times, where I needed exactly someone like her to talk to, who could understand what I felt. I am sure I cannot find a better person than her. She is the one who taught me the most valuable lesson in life. I never thought she would be a history in life where i was looking forward to getting into history together as the best couple ever.

Sun light flashed into my face. Oh! Wait! What did I do the entire night? I wet my bed for the first time after my childhood. But this time with tears, tears from my eyes signaled from the heart and mind informing that I have no place in her heart. I don't know how long it would take for me to be the way I used to before. It is not possible to be the same. Because before, it was only her. She was my life. She still is.

Early morning, it was too late to sleep. I had to get back to the office in three hours. I stood under the shower. My best friend at that point in time, as it helped me in wiping my tears, which were faster than the shower. I had never felt so lonely before. I asked her to call me when she is free. She called back immediately. I feel much better listening to her voice. She was happy. What else do I want?

"Are you sure this is what you want?" I asked. "Yes, and that's the reality. And you have to accept it", she said politely. I couldn't tell her how bad my situation was. I didn't want to bring her down. I told her to think wisely and take a decision, as it's a decision for a lifetime. And I also told "tell him that, if he breaks your heart, I'm gonna break his neck". "I'll tell him. That's so sweet of you", she said. "You are my Childu. You will always be my cute little Childu", I said. And I also was constantly asking her if she was very sure about this and how all this happened. She got *annoyed and said she'll talk to me tomorrow and cut the call.*

I felt a little better after talking to her. Because it is her life. And she is happy with her decision. I was still afraid of one thing. What if this doesn't work out for her?

I am very sure she won't be able to take the pain. She might not even tell me if anything goes wrong. Will she be able to deal with it? More than being depressed, I was afraid answering the above questions to myself. The battle of my heart and mind started again. But none of them won. Tears won. That was the only outcome of this complete process.

The next day she came to college, to collect her 2nd Puc marks sheet as she had completed her undergraduate course. She called me as she came. I came down to help her with the process. Once done we entered lift as I came along to drop her near her vehicle. "Want to have some coffee?", I asked. She said no. "Tea?" I asked. No, she said again. "Some juice?, I spontaneously responded. "Dude, if you want to have tell directly, we'll go", she said and pressed the lift button to the floor which had canteen. I took a coffee while she had coldbadam milk. We spoke a lot. Definitely not about us. We spoke and we spoke. I didn't want those conversations to end. Though we weren't talking anything important. She took a couple of biscuits from the front biscuits box that was kept which the canteen had. She paid for it. And she said "dude, he didn't see me taking biscuits. But if I don't pay him it'll be like cheating from my side and for him it will be like teaching a lesson".

She said that in a childish tone that melt my heart. She paid for all anyway. I wanted to go to center of the college and should 'Childu I love you". My emotions were like an iceberg. The tip was seen on top. But inside deep only I know how much of the pain I was going through.

I thought through this entire situation. Just a couple of days before she said about getting into a relationship, which she wasn't ready to. In fact, she wasn't ready to get into relationship at all. That was the reason she was single till now! I talked her through this, and I didn't even for a blue moon thought think that it would go against me. She also knows it very well that no one will ever love her as much as I love her!

It's a fourth day morning since she said that to me, and I haven't slept since then. I could not. My day ever since I met her would start by wishing her good morning, and wouldn't end without wishing her good night before I or she goes to sleep.

She is expecting me to end my life without her. She doesn't know that might be anytime now. 'Should I live without her?' that is not the question at all. 'Can I live without her?' never even think about it is the only answer. Is this the end? That's the only solution for me to get rid of the pain I am going through. The amount of pain my heart is bearing is beyond the worst possible. I couldn't for a second stop thinking about her.

To relieve my heart from the pain which I couldn't bear, I had to put an end. An end to me! Her presence in my life has had a huge impact that I cannot imagine a life without her. Yes, this is it. I cannot live without her!

Ending it all at once was all I was thinking about. The only ray of hope I had to live was that, what if she was kidding? What if she said that she is getting into a relationship just to put an end to my dream that I told her about how our future is going to be?

"Don't have so much plans of future with me, I don't think it would work out", she had told when I explained her how our future would be ahead together. She didn't want me to plan for her. Did she make up this whole getting into a relationship story just so that to put an end now no matter how hard it is rather that what she thought would end when the actual time comes?

What she doesn't know is that, no matter what, until death apart us, nothing can ever rip us apart.

I don't know how this thought came to me, but it did sound relevant. But she on the other hand doesn't know that this is the only thought and believe that has still kept my heart beating! She is the reason why my heart beats; there is no other reason for my heart to beat without her!

This is not the first time I cried. Yes, I have cried in the past, but hardly a few times, and never like this before. Yes, just like everyone did my life started with me cry, but I didn't expect it to also end with my cry. The first time I cried because of my mom, and that's the nature of any birth. The last time I cried is for her, and I myself didn't expect this to end it this way.

What if she wasn't kidding? She isn't the kind of girl who will make fun of serious situations. The reason for me to think that she was kidding was that she used to tell me everything. Every single thing! And how come she hadn't said me about this guy with whom she was about to fall in love. Our friendship was in such a stage that she would consider my advice for any single decision. But this, a life changing decision, wouldn't she have asked me if it was something this serious? Or had she already forgotten me?

For a while my entire life till now flashed in front of my eyes. Almost all the happy moment in those life memories had her presence. None of the saddest moments in the past were as depressing as I am today!

Talking to her would always help me, I called her. Her voice made me feel the excitement as if I was doing something new and interesting. "Can we go out this weekend, I asked. "No, I can't", she said. "I know I will never get to go out with you here after", I replied. "I didn't tell that", she replied. "I know Childu, I know it very well. Unless we run into each other accidently, I won't get a chance to meet you!" after hearing that, she replied, "May be". That was it. "All the best! Be happy forever! Take care!" I said and cut the call.

Was that all? It seemed so easy. But it was exactly the opposite. I couldn't control the flow of water in my eyes.

I used to call her Childu for a reason. For her childish behavior and nature. But just like a child she forgot everything in just a few seconds and move forward. For all the times we spent together, for all the conversations we had together, I never imagined that she would end this as easy as this. That was it! I never ever wanted to talk to her ever again. Because I knew that's what she wanted. I could always sense her thinking and thoughts just by listening to her voice, or by looking at her texts. I swear, nobody in this world would ever be able to understand her as much as I do! Why can't she understand that?

It hurts a lot when you show all the love you have for one person and not getting back even a percent back. I didn't have to take a chance of ending my life; she already killed me with her words.

That was the end of my anger towards her, I remembered her face and a smile automatically without even me realizing flashed on. I forgot why I was angry.

If I had to end everything with her, every feeling I had towards her, I had to end my life. Because she was my life!

'Five minutes! In five minutes I will stop breathing! Dear heart, just bear the pain for five last minutes!' I told myself. My phone started vibrating. Samartha's call. "Hey! Long time, want to catch up? My place now", he said. "I'm on my way", I said and left to his place.

Samartha knew everything about all this. He was one friend whom I would turn to for everything. I reached his place. I stood outside the door just to make sure to act normal and be normal. I knocked the door bell. As soon as he opened, I hugged him and broke down as I couldn't control my emotions rolling down in the form of tears. A friend's shoulder to wipe your tears is the best feeling in the world.

None of my friends or either anyone I know, have ever seen me like this. I would always be smiling. 'Smiling' was the prefix added to my name. Even when someone is scolding, I would be smiling. Samartha was shocked to see me like this. As I told. This was the first time I had ever loved someone so much in my entire life. I was very sure I would never love anyone as much as I loved Childu in my entire life hereafter. "I have seen you for a very long time, almost eight years. I have never seen you like this before. I know how you were before. I also know how you are after you met her. Your life has completely changed ever since you met her", Samartha said. I didn't have a voice to talk. What I am now, all the success in my life was only after I met Childu. Childu played a huge role in my life. The success I have is not my credit alone. I share the credits with her. She changed my life. Completely! Start-up a company of my own, a training and development venture, taking classes and sessions in college, a satisfying job and a well settled life. Everything came after she came into my life!

I was so into her that I had never even concentrated much towards my professional life. But that didn't affect any of my professional activities as it was my passion. Talking is something I love to do. Doing what you do the best for a living, hardly a few people are privileged. And everyone who has done it, are the most successful people!

I had no idea that I could be successful in this life. Whatever I did after she came into my life was all turning out to be the best outcome. I got everything after she came in my life, or rather she gave me everything in life, and just when I thought I had everything, she left!

Samartha tried to console me. He offered me a beer. I had quit drinking a couple of years ago. I knew if I started to drink again now, I would not stop for a long time and maybe it might lose all the success I have earned till now. I told him I will sleep for a while and went to bed.

Four days it had been already since I had slept. I still could not sleep. As soon as I hit the bed and close my eyes, I could only see her. It doesn't matter how worst I felt, I didn't want her to know what I was going through. All the last four days, I did talk to her. Yes, of course with a smile. Never ever show your pain to the person whom you love. I stopped talking to her for one reason. Not because she didn't want to ever meet me, but because I didn't want she to know if at all something happens to me.

My mind was filled with negative thoughts. From the day I first met her, till the day she said she will never meet me, were the days of my life. This will remain the best days of my life.

Getting emotionally attached to a person is the biggest curse.

It was one of such times, where I needed exactly someone like her, to talk to, who could understand what I felt. I am sure I cannot find a *better person than her. She is the one who taught me the most valuable lesson in life. I never thought she would be a history in life where I was looking forward to getting into history together as the best couple ever.*

Sun light flashed into my face. Oh! Wait! What did I do the entire night? I wet my bed for the first time after my childhood. But this time with tears, tears from my eyes signaled from the heart and mind informing that I have no place in her heart. I don't know how long it would take for me to be the way I used to before. It is not possible to be the same. Because before, it was only her. She was my life. She still is.

Early morning, it was too late to sleep. I had to get back to the office in three hours. I stood under the shower. My best friend at that point in time, as it helped me in wiping my tears, which were faster than the shower. I had never felt so lonely before. I asked her to call me when she is free. She called back immediately. I feel much better listening to her voice. She was happy. What else do I want?

"Are you sure this is what you want?" I asked. "Yes, and that's the reality. And you have to accept it", she said politely. I couldn't tell her how bad my situation was. I didn't want to bring her down. I said her to think wisely and take a decision, as it's a decision for a lifetime. And I also told "tell him that, if he breaks your heart, I'm gonna break his neck". "I'll tell him. That's so sweet of you", she said. "You are my Childu. You will always be my cute little Childu", I said. And I also was constantly asking her if she was very sure about this and how all this happened. She got annoyed and said she'll talk to me tomorrow and cut the call.

I felt a little better after talking to her. Because it is her life. And she is happy with her decision. I was still afraid of one thing. What if this doesn't work out for her? I am very sure she won't be able to take the pain. She might not even tell me if anything goes wrong. Will she be able to deal with it? More than being depressed, I was afraid answering the above questions to myself. My heart's and mind's battle started again. But none of them won. Tears won. That was the only outcome of this complete process.

I used to get calls from Meena at least once in a week. But after that incident where she saw me, I started getting calls from her every now and then. I just used to cut the call and ignore. But at that point in time when she called, I don't know why, I answered. "Hello", I spoke. She called my name. "Yes, tell me", I replied. "I want to talk to you, can we meet", I heard from her side. "I am really not in the mood Meena", I said and I thought of cutting the call. But still I held up. If I am going through all this. Maybe if she had a reasonable explanation, she might have also gone through all this. I wondered and said I'll meet her in about an hour in the coffee shop.

She didn't start explaining, instead she saw me with an unusual face. I would always be smiling no matter what. But that was the situation where my face had completely forgotten how to smile. "What's wrong?", she asked. "Nothing", I said. Though everything was wrong. "Hey, you can share it with me; I'm still your friend." she said in a soft voice. "You are always my friend Meena, but I had asked you not to do one thing, to apologize no matter what, but you did that, when I was expecting a relevant answer", I said. She looked at me and said, "Yes, the guy whom you saw me with is my sister's friend. My sister ran away with her boyfriend and I had to find her. He knew where she was. I could not tell this then. Family issues you know. How to spread. So I told you my mom wasn't well and went with him to get her back", she explained. "What happened?" I asked. "The guy cheated my sister and left her all alone, I convinced her to come back. And now she is married and happy", she said. "I am sorry", I replied. "The rule applies to you as well, no apologies, no matter what", she quickly said with a sarcastic smile. "I am sorry", I said again and smiled.

I then realized how important it will be to hear out from people. It doesn't matter what or how big the mistake it is. I made a promise to myself to give a chance to explain. "How you been? What happened? Why are you not looking good?", Meena put in a series of questions. I said her about what all happen between me and Childu. "Do you love her so much?" Meena asked. "Yes", I said as I was almost about to break down. Yes, I think I almost did. We were about to leave, and Meena said, "Dude, if you want to talk to someone, I am always there". I just smiled, and we left.

The next day Childu came to college, to collect her 2nd Puc mark sheet as she had completed her undergraduate course. She called me as she came. I came down to help her with the process. Once done, we entered the lift as I came along to drop her near her vehicle. "Want to have some coffee?", I asked. She said no. "Tea?" I asked. No, she said again. "Some juice? I spontaneously responded. "Dude, if you want to have tell directly, we'll go", she said, and pressed the lift button to the floor which had canteen. We had watermelon Juice. I, as usual was playing around and talking to her about what all would happen if we had got married. But she was all like, "Dudee, stop it dudeee, you know that's not going to happen. Why to talk about it?" The routine again continued after we had Juice. We went to the place where her Dio was parked and she dropped me back near the entrance. *"Bye Childu, drive safe"*, I said. *"Bye"*, she waved and left.

I still could not sleep. I wanted to meet her badly to talk about what all is currently going on. I knew I wouldn't have gotten proper answers from her. But still I wanted to talk to her. I dropped in a text to her, *"Childu, one last meet. For one last time, let's go out. I want you to be with me for an entire day"*. She read the message but didn't reply then. I waited for a long time. It was evening, around 4 PM I sent her the text followed by, *"Please. One last meet"*. She might have thought that would be the last time we both would meet. But what she probably wouldn't know is that, it would be the last time I would ever meet someone!

It was 8 PM and I still didn't receive any message or call from her. 10 PM, she sent me a text, *"Ok"*. *"Next weekend?"* I replied. As I had to work the entire week and could not take a day off. *"Ok"*, she sent again. I knew on some level I had already lost her. Her cute childish attitude which was the main reason I fell in love with her at the first place. I finally after four days slept for a while.

My schedule ever since I met her included texting and talking to her all the time. I knew that would not be happening hereafter. I could not take that either.

The meanwhile my professional life got a huge turnaround. Commencement of academic year. I had to go to each and every PUC, B.COM and MBA classes to take orientation classes. Introducing all the aspiring students to the college and warmly welcoming them. I also got an opportunity to teach a subject for B.com students. That was my life passion. But without life, I couldn't concentrate on passion alone.

I am a motivational speaker. But that was something I lacked at that point in time. I had lost all the hope to live. In that tough situation, I would still go to classes and inspire students to be successful in life. Yes, I had success in life, but I didn't have a life in success. When I meant life, it's her!

You can't go to a class or talk to students with a dull face. Should always be smiling. Where could I find smile? When my entire smile was with her. Which I know I won't get. It was hard to maintain a fake smile all the time. "Hey, what happened to you?", someone asked. That was the hundredth time people in college had asked me. I didn't know what to reply. I just got used to smile and walk away.

I was sitting in a staff room where a group of students came to meet me. "Hi sir, we really liked your session. We would love to have more and more of such sessions", a guy who attended my session said. "That is really heartwarming to listen, I will definitely meet you guys again", I replied. "Thank you sir", they said and left. That's what a profession like mine would look for. I couldn't be happy for long, as the pain in my heart would only remind me of Childu.

Every time I took a walk in the campus. I would see students who would be wanting to tell me hi and greet with a smile. My students smile would help me to heel my pain, but just for seconds. There is a difference between having everything in life and having what you want. That difference was her. There is also a difference between ending my life with her and without her.

With her it would be a lifetime. Without her, it's anytime now. That was my mindset.

Samartha came down to my office during lunch time. He forced me to go out for lunch with me. We went to have Biryani. As we reached there, "This is the place where she and I had come out for lunch for the first time", I said. "Shut up, don't talk about it now. Just eat", he said. I saw the table where I and Childu were sitting. I couldn't stop picturing us in that table. That was the first time I had come out with her. Thinking about that day and those memories, I finished up an entire Biryani. That was the first proper meal I had since the last few days.

I came back to college and went to take the last class of the day. After the class, a guy came up to me, "sir, I am looking for an internship. Can you help me with it?". "Yes, definitely. I'll keep you posted if anything comes up", I said, as I was also looking after placements too.

A friend of mine called and said a girl wanted to meet me for personality and soft skills development. I asked him to send her to college. I spoke to her for about thirty minutes in the college canteen. "Thank you so much, your talks meant a lot. It'll definitely help me", she said and left. I still sat there alone for an hour. What am I doing? I am helping people. Is there anyone who can help me? Yes, it's Childu. Being a motivational speaker, I did lack in motivation for myself.

Every time I opened my whatsapp, I could see her whatsapp profile picture. That would kill me every time. Luckily, I haven't broken my phone yet. Her smile and her beautiful eyes were stuck in my heart, which I am sure can never be separated. If it has to be separated. It has to come out along with my heart.

I couldn't wait to meet her. I knew it would be the last time I would ever meet her. I was as excited as I was waiting to meet her for the first time, outside the college seminar hall for the Kannada event. I knew it would be the last time I could meet her. I didn't want today to end at all. White round neck t-shirt, a black jeans and a blue blazer was my attire for the second last trip of my life. The last trip is undoubtedly to the place where nobody can find me forever!

8 AM in the morning, I went to a temple near her home. Where she said she would meet me at 9 AM. I stepped out of my car. She came out of the temple wearing a blue salvar and jeans. As natural and as beautiful as she always is. "You said you'll come at 9 AM", I asked. "I knew you would be here early", she said. "I'll drive", she said, and took the wheels. "As you say, madam", I replied and sat inside the car. "Long drive?" she asked. Why would I say no to that? "Let's go", I said. As we hit the highway, she accelerated to top speed. She loves cars, especially riding. Unlike the other girls who likes something that is pink or a Barbie.

She looked so happy riding the car. She opened the window. The air made her hair fly, so did my heart. I was only looking at her. She turned at me. "See road and drive", I said. "I know, I've seen the road, it won't change", she said and made a funny face. She saw a board, 'Biryani' and stopped the car. Just like old times, Biryani buddies were back. I said to me, 'this would probably be the last time I will have Biryani with her'. We had Biryani and continued our journey.

"Do you have any idea where we are going?" I asked. *"No dude, road is good. Let's keep going",* she said. *"All roads till the end won't be the same",* I said looking at her. She saw me and replied, *"I know. But you will never reach the destination if you don't take chance",* she said sensing the topic changing. I didn't tell anything. *"Dude, don't be like this",* she said and parked the car. It was a lovely place, fully greenery around. *"Let's not talk about this now",* I said. *"Not just now, let's ever talk about this again",* she said and asked, *"Is it okay?"* I nodded my head gesturing yes, a half hearted nod it was.

We left the car there and started walking. We could hear our footsteps while walking. I had nothing to cover up the silence. *"Dude",* she called. *"Listen",* she said. She saw me nodding and continued, *"It doesn't work out between us, we'll remain the best of best and closest friends there ever could be. I do love you..."* I interrupted while she said that, *"That's enough for me! I love you more Childu..."* yeah! It was her turn now to interrupt and she went on, *"I love you as a friend. But nothing beyond that",* she said. I did not have a choice, "Okay, remember, I am always there for you", I said. "I know", She said.

We continued to walk, not towards the car. I was thinking 'How far?'. Did she forget that we also have to walk back towards the car again to continue our ride?

Once in a lifetime, you meet someone who takes your breath away. Not because you want them too, but because they were meant to, and that person will change your life forever. She was the one who took my breath away in the first meet. And she probably is taking it forever in her last meet.

We almost walked a kilometer. I don't know what she was thinking. Surrounding was completely covered with mountains and greenery. We could hear water flowing, a few steps further both of us turned toward left and saw an amazing river flowing. We walked towards the river between the woods. It was 100 meters from the main road we were walking. She almost slipped near the river side; she held my shoulder tight for support to avoid falling. Our eyes met each other, both the eyes knew they were in love with each other, but she hid that for what reason only she knows.

We sat by the river side for an hour without talking. Sun was slowly going to sleep. She slowly leaned on to my shoulders and said, "I don't want to lose you forever". I got to know, her reason for not accepting my love was not because she doesn't love me or because she loves someone else, which I very well know she completely made up. There must be a strong reason for her to not accept my love. "I will never lose you Childu, unless you forget me", I replied. She stood up and said, "I won't and I can't forget you". I turned towards her and was looking at her. She started walking towards the main road.

As we reached near the car, moon was in the background; my car was a little further. It looked as if we were walking in moonlight towards the car. The best walk I ever had. Not just the walk, the life I had after her entry, was the best!

It was dark and I didn't want her to ride. I took the wheels. "I am hungry", she said as we sat *inside the car. I was pretty sure there was nothing available around 20 kilometers radius. I knew she wanted Biryani again for dinner. We stopped at a dhaba after 25 kilometer ride. "Biryani again?" I asked. "Yes, obviously!" she replied and got down. We had a Biryani and a lime soda each. "What next?" I asked. "You tell sir", she questioned back. "Are you sure you'll do whatever I tell then?" I asked. "Ayee, come let's get back home", she replied.*

We got back in the car to get back home. On our way back, she said, "Thank you for everything". I couldn't hide tears in my eyes as they rolled down; I couldn't see her face to face. Shockingly, she too did cry at the same time. "No Childu, Thank you for everything", I replied as I stopped in front of her house. "Bye, Good Night", she said. "You too Childu", I said and took off.

It was 11:30 as I reached home. I hit the bed as soon as I reached home. But couldn't sleep. My pillow blamed eyes for wetting it, eyes blamed heart for the same, and heart had no reason to take the blame for falling in love at the first place. My entire body wanted heart to stop its function, but failed to understand that if heart stops, that's the end to the rest as well. I still wanted to end; I didn't know what else to do. I couldn't live without her. Life is so weird when it comes to taking decisions at a certain situation. Even though when we have a right thought and a right decision, the wrong thought and wrong decisions seem to me more apt to the situation to choose. That's when we do really have to be careful in choosing one.

I was afraid of choosing! A decision. I completely left it to fate and go on with the flow of whatever happens. I didn't bother much to whatever happened. But I couldn't forget her memories in my life.

You do know,
That I can't live without you.
You do know,
How much I love you.
You do know,
How much you mean to me!
You do know,
How much I want you to be with me.

For You From Me!

You do know,
How hard it is to imagine life without YOU!

The sound of crying has spread in the air for a
while,
The heart that has lost all the time is quite.
Life is not a game,
To find a reason to blame.
Should I laugh with all the pain?
Should I cry with the memories that I gain

I still love you,
I wanted to shout.
But by then I knew,
Your heart had thrown me out.
I had no choice,
Though it was nice.
I had to choose between you and my life.
That was when I understood,
YOU ARE MY LIFE!

It was 4:00 AM in the morning and I still didn't have a hint of feeling sleepy. I wondered if I should put an end to all and rest in peace forever. I could only remember the times I spent with Childu and nothing else. Her smile, her looks, her attitude and the way she acted around me; I couldn't think of anything else.

It was 7:00 AM already. I had no interest to do anything. I was wondering of going on a long ride and never coming back. I freshened up and my phone beeped. It was an unknown number.

It reads:

"Dear Sir,

Thank you for helping me with my placement training, soft skills and motivating me. I have a job interview today. Wish me luck".

"All the best ma. Do call me and let me know the results at the end of the day", I replied.

It brought a big smile on my face. I completely forgot about why I was depressed. Yes, I am a motivational speaker, I motivate people. I help people. This is what I am. I don't need someone to motivate me. I am motivation myself. I did not even know the name of the person who texted me. I felt so proud of myself. I was as happy as I ever was.

Childu came in my life and left. That doesn't mean the end of everything. There are so many lives that I've touched, so many students whom I inspire. I have to live for them; I should never stop inspiring people. This is what I am meant to do. This is what I should do.

I waited till evening, waiting for a call from that student who sent that text in the morning. It was 6:40 PM, I got a call. "Hello sir, I got selected", she said. "Congratulations", I said. "What's your name by the way?", I asked. "Anushree sir", she replied. "Oh ya! I remember", I said. "How was the interview?", I questioned. "Good sir, your suggestions really helped me a lot", she said wit happiness. "I will meet you tomorrow in college sir, thank you so much", she said. "Good Night ma, see you tomorrow", I said. Tears rolled out of my eyes! This time, it was tears of happiness.

Samartha called and asked if I was free to meet. "Yes, definitely yes. I'm coming to your place", I said and went to meet him. I went to his place. "What happened? You look so happy?" he asked. I said him about everything. He got pretty mad at me for the thought of ending my life. But then he said, "You are an inspiration maga, so proud of you". He gave me a hug, a best friend forever hug.

We went out for dinner. Meena accompanied us. "What's up dude?" Meena asked. "All good Meena. How's everything going on with you?", I asked. "All fine", she said. "Vishal, Raghu and Ruthuparna are busy with some work and can't make it", said Samartha. We had dinner, for a change, I had fried rice instead of Biryani. Life is not just about one preference. There are different options available for everyone who we will only not know whether we will like it or not. Once we were done, we were leaving. Meena came with me as I said I'll drop her home. We stopped for a desert on our way.

"Dude, I want to talk to you", she said. "No, Meena. I think I know what you want to talk.

But I'm not ready for anything. I hope Samartha already told you what happen", I replied gently. She didn't tell anything. "I am sorry dude; I am not in a position to talk about anything. You are the sweetest girl I know. But I am not in that situation to complicate anything. I just want to concentrate on my career and move forward without thinking about any obstacles in my way. Sorry", I said. "I know dude, sorry. No matter what, if you feel like talking to someone, I am always there", she said. I just smiled.

Those were the exact words I had earlier said to Childu. 'No matter what, if you feel like talking to someone, I am always there'. Life is strange, isn't it? You move out of your comfort zone to make feel comfortable with you, in the meanwhile there will be someone else who will be turning towards you to make you feel comfortable. I felt really happy for that. I was happy for another reason too. That I was so matured that I was able to think about all this from another angle as well. 'There is life, there is life even after all, the worst that could happen to you', I thought to myself as I dropped Meena to her home. "Good Night Meena",

I said. "Good Night, take care", she said as I took off.

I went home and thought about what all went wrong. I could only find my mistakes.

I am hurt only because of me, nobody else has the power to hurt you except you! It's only you who can hurt yourself to the extent that nobody can ever imagine. The first mistake I ever did in terms of hurting myself was to fall in love! If I hadn't fallen in love, I wouldn't have been hurt this much to this extent. But I cannot blame love for what happened to me it was destiny! It was destined to happen this way! I cannot blame anyone except me for what happened to me because it is what I chose for me if it had turned the other way around then I wouldn't have anything to blame that is because I trust myself for certain situations which were not in my control. The second mistake I was not considering what her opinion could have been. It is not her mistake to reject me; it is my fault for expecting something that I could not ever get. I still did not know how I thought about all this. I am still worried about how and where this whole situation is going to *leave me. Yes, I am depressed; I am depressed on the current situation I am in. It is what I decided for myself! Nobody Else had planned this situation for me; this is a situation where I put myself in. Can I get out of it? It's a question mark. It's always going to be a question mark!*

I did have a decent amount of sleep that night. It is not because I was ok with the complete situation, it was because I was able to understand that the situation I was in, which was created by me. I was the one to have been blamed for whatever happened. The next day morning I went to college, Anushree was supposed to meet me during her break time.

It was 9:00 A.M. in the morning when I had no class and I was sitting in the canteen. I could see people everywhere around happily talking and laughing. I felt as if everyone in the world is happy except me! But I had no one to blame for that it was all what I made for myself. I wanted to get out of it, but Childu had a huge impact in my life that it was unable to get over her. If things were right, if everything have been, as I thought it would be, Childu would have been the Love of My

Life and I would have had the best life anyone could have ever imagined.

I still believe if Childu had said yes! My life today would have been completely different. But I could sense that Childu will never ever come in my life again. I just had to forget her and move forward in life. I had a life, I had a better life. This is not what I am. This is not how I am supposed to be. I was so happy yesterday evening when I got to know I actually helped a student of mine in shaping her career. This is why I have to live; this is what I have to do for the rest of your life. I love to do this. I will do this for the rest of my life without any regret or expectations.

The principal of college was on rounds. He came to the canteen where I was sitting. He came up to me and asked, "How is everything going on everything?", "Has to be fine sir, if not life cannot move on. For life to move, on even though everything isn't fine, we have to see to that we at least react as if everything is fine", I said he saw me for a couple of seconds without uttering a word and replied, "Sometimes it is very hard to understand whatever you say but it always make sense of whatever you say even if we are not able to understand it", he just walked away.

I sat in the canteen till the break time, Anushree came up to me, she said "Thank you so much sir, you really helped me a lot", "I am glad I could help congratulations with your job, I am sure you will do Great all the best", I said. She brought me a cup of coffee, she bought one for herself as well. "Sir frankly speaking, at first when I saw you I never thought your session would help me so much, sir, thank you so much", she said and left after finishing the coffee as it was time for her class.

I feel so happy inside, but I couldn't show that outside. I could still feel the pain inside me the pain which at that moment I thought would never heal the only medicine I could find for the pain were smiles! Smiles of people whom I could help smile!

Whatever I do, reminded me of Childu. I was so used to talking and chatting with her all day long. I used to update her every single minute thing that used to happen. And so did her. I missed her badly. *After doing something, I without my realization would dial her number or open her whatsapp to talk to her about the same. And then I would realize that she is no longer in my life. That situation would break my heart all the time.*

Though I was not worried or thinking about what I lost, a thought entered my mind which automatically to me, back to the situation, the same situation which was very hard to come out of. I was only thinking about me and my situation, but I never thought that what she was going through? What was on her head even though I knew she love me? But there's something that was stopping her from saying that to me. There could be a lot of answers to that question. I wanted to hear that from her, but I knew she wouldn't tell me. I wanted to meet her and ask what was wrong. Why didn't she want this to happen? But as I had told her earlier that the last meet of ours would be the last time we ever meet, I didn't want to break that. But that was something I badly wanted to know. I badly wanted to hear from her. It is so unsettling to not to know answers to a certain question which could change your life for a better tomorrow. I didn't even know if I could work out on what she things would not work out. This could have been the happiest endings in both of our lives. I really badly wanted to ask Childu to meet me for one last time again to ask about what was wrong, what went wrong and where she thought it would not work out.

This thought came to me after a week. A week after I thought I could move on with life and live without her. How could I live without her when she was my life? I thought of calling her! Exactly that time I got a call from her! She said "Hello", I broke down as soon as I heard her voice after a week. That was something my ears were waiting to listen. Her voice! I heard her voice after a week. She did not talk anything after 'Hello', I didn't know should I talk or should I wait for her to talk. "How are you Childu?" I asked. "I am fine. How are you?" she replied. "I think it's going on fine," I said in a very low tone. She even sensed that what I said was completely opposite. "I feel like having Biryani" she said. I couldn't resist, I couldn't control the Tears in my eyes. This time tears of happiness. I went to her place as quick as possible. Just like previous times, Biryani buddies, we are back again. We had Biryani. I didn't ask her anything. Though, I had a lot in my mind to ask. She didn't talk anything. Though, she had a lot in her mind to talk. It was a complete a silent Biryani date.

We were walking on the road once we had completed eating. She spoke! She finally spoke about what I wanted to know. "Dude, I know you know that I don't have a boyfriend or I love anybody else. I know it very well that you know that I am sorry for saying that. I told that only for one reason because you had huge hopes on me and our future together. I just wanted you to break that hope and move forward in life. I am hundred percent sure that it's not going to happen even though I want it to happen. I am really sorry I cannot help it," she said, all at a time. As if she had by hearted. I did not tell anything. In fact, I could not and I didn't want to tell anything. While she continued, she said "I have promised my mom that I will marry whomever she asks me to. I don't want to break the promise that I made to her. Her entire life, she had taken a good care of me. I lost my dad at a very young age. All my mom gave her complete life just for care of mine, and until now there hasn't been a single thing that she did not give me. She has given me everything she has sacrificed her entire life for me and I don't want to hurt her by doing anything that even has a slight possibility of hurting her."

I was speechless. I didn't know how to react. We were still walking down the road. It was an Empty Road. "Not just that" she continued, "Even if my mom agrees, you know right Indian families. They think a lot dude. They talk a lot. Especially about other's family. If I ever do something wrong people in family do not talk about me, they talk about my upbringing, my mom. I don't want that to happen. I won't let that happen. I know people make talk today and forget tomorrow. But when people talk something bad, that would be something my mom would regret forever. And if I make my mom regret, that would make me regret forever. I know I have taken a right decision and I hope you understand. I hope we can be good friends forever. My intention is not to hurt you. My only intention is not to hurt anybody else because of my decision." she said. "I am sorry. Your mom is so lucky to have you as a daughter." I told her.

And that is in fact true. She had a point! A valid point. In fact, as much as I love her, I also respect her decision. That automatically comes when you love someone truly. It is not just about loving a person and willing to spend the rest of the life without them. It is also so important to let the person you love live the life the way they want it to be. Your loved ones happiness should be your happiness. That is love!

I dropped Childu back home. She didn't even turn back to tell bye. She walked away with tears in her eyes!

I felt like talking to Meena. I called Meena and ask her if she was free to meet. She said that meet me in the same place where we used to meet earlier. I told her about what happened and I asked her was my decision correct. She obviously couldn't say no. "You did the right thing" she said.

As Meena knew my situation, she did not express what I could see in her eyes. I could see in her eyes what Childu could see in my eyes when I was with her. Love! I did not know whether I did the right thing or not in the past, leaving the one who loves me and going behind the one where there was no future with. Meena did not tell anything about her feelings because she knew what I would tell and what I would tell, would definitely hurt her feelings. She is not ready for that, and I was not ready to hurt her as well. "Should I be happy for letting my loved one be happy or should I be sad for sacrifice in my happiness" I asked Meena. She said in very simple words "You will be happy. No doubt about it. You might be hurt, but imagine tomorrow when the real time comes when your loved one's thought or relationship not working out becomes true; it will be a hundred times harder than this. And you will be hundred times more hurt than how much hurt you are today. That small happiness, what you have from letting your loved one be happy will be hundred times happier tomorrow for the same reason. You will definitely find someone with whom you are destined to end your life with". I felt so happy listening to Meena I told her "Thank you so much Meena. Your words *means a lot, it really does. Thanks!" I said as we took off.*

Just like all guys do after every breakup, it's a mandatory party time. Samartha, Vishal, Raghu and Ruthu were waiting for me. It was one of the best times indeed. Best Friends Forever in such situations make a lot of difference. All the things they tell you to make you feel comfortable. It's a known fact that you don't actually care for whatever they tell, but still, it means a lot. Not because they said that, it is because you know you have someone to tell that. It is God's gift. Such friends in life, they are very few. Never lose them.

Well, I got so drunk. I started abusing love. I know it's not right. But that's why actually people drink after breakup. To enjoy that feeling of abusing love. It's my time, and I really had a very good time. We woke up the next day morning and could hardly recollect what we did last night. We definitely did something fishy last night, but none of us really remember what we did. We were all trying to recollect while Samartha and Ruthu were still sleeping. I checked my call list and messages to confirm that I did not call or text Childu. Which, thankfully I did not do. Then what the hell did we do? "I had a dream that we were all roaming in the road searching for liquor store" said Samartha, has he just woke up. "Hey! That is not a dream! I repeat that is not a dream. I think we did that", Vishal said. "Yeah, we ran out of liquor while we were drinking and we went down to get some. But after that I do not recollect anything that we did. What did we do?" Raghu asked. "I don't know", I said. We all were wondering what happened and what we did last night while Raghu was still sleeping. All that we remember was we drank, we spoke, abused love, we ran out of drink and hence we went down to get some drink! That is all what we remember. And after that something happened. But we do not know what happened. We couldn't figure out as well.

Raghu woke up. In fact, he did not, but Samartha accidentally kicked him, which woke him up. As soon as he woke up "did you talk to her", he asked me. "What?" we all were shocked at the same time and ask him to whom should we talk to and what should we talk?" "Last night you called Meena. Remember? And you told her you love her.

I think you made the right decision. She asked you to call back tomorrow. You still didn't call her? I thought the first thing you would do as soon as you wake up was to call her!" Rughu said. I was completely shocked and so were Raghu, Vishal and Samartha. I did not believe initially. "I just saw my phone and checked my contacts and messages. I had not done anything that silly" I said. Rughu replied that Meena had called him last night to check whether I was fine and Rughu handed over the phone to me which he should not have been done! Because I was not in my senses firstly, and secondly, why the hell did he do that? I questioned myself.

I didn't want to call Meena. Maybe she told to call back tomorrow because she got to know that I was drunk. It was quite obvious because probably the way I would have spoken might have made her tell the she will talk tomorrow, if not she should have definitely told yes last night only. I heard the conversation on the phone which was recorded by the true recorder in Ruthu's phone. I definitely sounded a lot drunk than I thought I was! I wondered, should I call Meena now and apologize for what happened. I thought of not calling at all. It was already almost afternoon, Meena, herself called me. I didn't know whether to answer the call or not or whether to apologize as soon as I answer or not. But I had to pick up the call to at least tell her something. I thought of telling her the truth that I was drunk and I was not in my senses while I was talking to her. That would have made me a complete fool and created a bad impression on me. Thank God she didn't ask anything, but she asks me to meet. That was even worst, as I had to confess face to face. 'Meena listen" I said. "Let's meet and talk over it", she said, and cut the call.

What the hell did just happen, I thought to myself. Did she actually think that I really proposed or did she get to know that I was drunk or the worst possible situation was, if she thought that I was drunk and using her as a tool to get over Childu. I was so tense to meet Meena. But I had to meet her to clear all the confusion and to sort it out. I had no choice. I went to the coffee shop where we usually meet. Meena was there before me "Hi", I said. "What's up sir", she asked.

"Nothing much, but..." she stopped me while I was talking. "You don't have to tell anything dude. I love you too. I didn't want to tell this in phone. I wanted to tell you this in person so that I could see your expression. My expression! I thought to myself. What expression? This was completely a confused look expressions. She wanted to see that? That was something that I actually shouldn't be worrying about right now. Should I tell her the truth or continue with the lie? What was I supposed to do? I knew I didn't love her. But I could see her love for me in her eyes, though I did not love her, I said "I love you" I also said her "I am not sure if I am doing the right thing or not, I just came out of a situation that I couldn't imagine myself in. But I can see how much you care for me or how much you love me, in your eyes. That is the only reason for me to tell this." She was so happy. And I felt so happy too. Yes man, there are people who want you to be in their life. Live for them rather than thinking only about people whom you want to be in your life. Life is beyond that! Life is beyond everything. Whatever you think or whatever you want, might not come to you. But

what is destined for you and what you get after losing something is something that is better or even the best that what you have chosen for you.

Meena and I start meeting every day after that. She seems to be lot more interesting than what I thought her to be. I was just wondering the same thing over and over. Yes, I was lost! I was lost in someone else so much that I did not realize that on the other hand, there was someone who wanted me to be in her life. Though I was completely drunk when I said Meena that I love her, it was completely worth it. I did the right thing. I even told her about this. "Meena, I am sorry", I started. "Why?" she asked. "I thought we had a deal that neither of us apologizing to each other", she continued. "I did something really wrong that I had to apologize", I replied. "I don't think you did something wrong", she said. "I was completely drunk when I first told you I love you. And later I came to the Coffee shop to confess the same, but I saw the love in your eyes and I said I love you too, not because I loved you, but because I saw the love in your eyes and now I'm really happy that I did that. If not, I would have missed you.

I'm really sorry", I said. "Chill dude. Samarth already told me that. And he also told me that you already said him that you are going to confess to me. I'm so glad I called Rughu that day to check on how you were doing. Really, I am glad! And stop apologizing as you said there shouldn't be apologizing between us. I love you!" she said. "I love you too Meena" I said.

Happiness is not a choice, but being happy is a choice. You cannot choose happiness, but you can choose where and how to be happy. Every incident in life can turn out to be a complete life changer. Life changes if you make a choice. Or even if you don't make a choice there are various other choices in life. Choosing a choice isn't a game. It is not so important to choose the right one or the wrong one. It is important if you trust yourself and promise to be happy with whatever you choose. That is more than enough to keep you happy for the rest of your life.

Which Meena I knew in college days was completely different from which Meena I know today. Back then, since I was lost in another person everyone else were the same to me except that one special person. But that special person taught me the most valuable lessons in life that not everyone is the same. If you are including everyone; it also includes that one special person, if not every individual has their own individuality which can be bought out only when you explore it.

In one or the other way I never forgot Child. She taught me a lot of things in life. She taught me how to live life. Whatever I am today is what she shape me. I never knew I would be successful in life if she had not been in my life. I do not know if Meena had been in my life before Childu, if Childu wouldn't even have come in my life, would I have been this successful? That still remains as a question mark! Maybe Childu was supposed to come in my life just to teach me this lesson and Meena has come into my life to teach another lesson. But I am really glad and happy about how things are going on in my life as of now. And I may miss people and even people may miss me, but life has to go on. I can't miss days in life. Life has to continue.

It was Meena's birthday and it was a perfect plan to surprise her. Early morning as soon as she woke up in a bed me, Samartha, Vishal, Raghu and a couple of her friends Shweta and Pooja went to her place. As soon as she woke up she saw a huge human size teddy bear right in front of her where I was hiding behind. She was so excited she was so happy! I couldn't hide myself for long as I wanted to see her expression and I came out. She was even more surprised than I thought she would be. Her room was filled with balloons and she couldn't step down. In fact, she did not want to step down as she did not want to hurt balloons. She laughed! She laughed like a kid. I was very happy to be the reason for her happiness on her day. "Thank you so much" she said out loud, give me a hug. It meant a lot more to me. She introduced us to her parents. Surprisingly, she introduces me as her boyfriend! Her parents were shocked to listen to her tell that! And I definitely felt a little uncomfortable in that situation. But none of us me, Meena or her parents reacted much at that particular time and we moved on from that moment.

We all went out for lunch. We had a good time Meena and I came out separately after that. I asked Meena "What the hell was that in your home today? Why did you tell that?" She replied "Dude chill. There is nothing to hide. This is what I want. If not now, maybe some other day I will have to tell about the same thing. I don't want to hide it. I don't want to take it to the last moment. So, I just said off. I don't know if they liked that. Let's see if I go home now I will get to know everything." She said. "I love you Meena", I replied. I dropped her back home and I was eagerly waiting for her phone call later.

I do not know what conversation happened in her home. But I did not get the call or message from Meena for almost 2 hours. I was waiting. I had nothing else to do. It was not just Meena's future. It was also about my future too. I was also wondering if it goes out well, there it will be my chance next to speak up in my home regarding the same. I did not want to lose Meena. I knew that, my heart knew that and the fear in me that was wondering and worrying about what discussion is going on in our home now that. And finally, after 2 hours she called me "Dude, what do you think?" she asked. "Do you think I actually think?" I replied. "Dude tell no", she asked. "What should I tell ma?" I asked. "What do you think might have happened in my home? What do you think could be the result of the discussion?" she questioned. "I don't know. You tell me. Should I be worried?" I asked. "Can you come home now?" she questioned. "Do you want me to?" I asked again. "Yes", she replied. "Give me half an hour. I will be there", I said and I went to her home. She opened the door. All the way down there I was completed tense on what might have happened, but as soon as I saw her all my fear completed washed off, as she was smiling. And that smile gesturing everything was fine. I went inside and her parents started questioning me about me. It was not really like a tense question answer session like a teacher asking a student. It was like talking to new friends and getting to know each other. I was glad that there were no complications involved. On the other hand, I was worried that she has already done her part. And I still have to do mine. Are you kidding me? Me talking to my parents about my love! I was so scared. But I wanted to do it. If not for me, I had to do it for her.

I wanted to talk to my parents about this as soon as I reached home. But I couldn't. I don't know how to talk about this, but I did know that I have to talk about it. I went to my mom and I said that I am in love and I wanted her to meet her. She said okay. Let's go to her home and invite officially for a marriage proposal. I was shocked! I had prepared for at least 3 to 4 hours of conversation and it ended in less than a minute. I asked mom to check if it was okay to call her home so that mom would meet her first and then we can go to her home. Mom said "No, it is fine. The bride is not supposed to see the groom's home before marriage. We know what your choice is. We trust your choice, let's go and officially invite them this weekend."

Now I was wondering did I completely misunderstand my parents. I thought parents would be like villains in the movies. They are actually the sweetest aren't they?

The following weekend I and my family went to Meena's home. She was dressed up in blue saree. That was the first time I saw Meena in saree. She looked so beautiful. I fell in love with her all over again. She bought coffee to everyone. As that was a tradition. The girl has to get coffee for the guy and his family who has come for marriage proposal, so that the guy can hide and see her. The funny part is that, in that situation, everyone will have an eye on the guy. As in he is looking at the girl or not. It makes so difficult for the guy to actually look at the girl properly. She went back to the kitchen after serving. I wanted to see her again. I wantedly asked for some more sugar. She came again with sugar and she went back. I wanted to see her again. I again ask for some more sugar, this time for my mom. I did that again, asking sugar for my dad. Meena's dad asked Meena to stay in the hall to help me find no more excuses to call her. He looked at me and smiled. I smile back, gesturing Thank You.

I and Meena went outside to talk actually. In such situations, it is supposed to be parents who give privacy for newly to be couples to talk. But here it was a different situation. We both came out to give our parents' privacy to plan for our wedding and the next step to take it forward from here for the wedding. I said Meena "You look beautiful. You are the most beautiful girl in the world as of now. I'll promise you one thing; I will never hurt you or do anything that would hurt you. You are my princess and you will always be one". "Thank you", she replied and continued "Do you actually mean that or you are telling it for formality sake". "Dude, I said that for formality only. What now?" I asked. "Go and cancel the wedding if you want", I continued she became silent for a while and she seemed to be a little upset "Meena, I was just kidding. Nothing in the world actually means more than you to me. I just told I would ever never hurt you and If this joke really did hurt you, I'm sorry I'll never hurt you again I love you", I said. She gave me a hug and said "I love you too".

What is love?

Love is a magical feeling created between two people who are willing to spend the rest of their life together, caring for each other no matter what, being there for each other in whatever tough situation, trusting each other no matter what, believing in love which they created for them self.

Not everyone you lose is a loss. The reality is, you didn't lose anything and what you think is loss is actually your gain. You need to stop worrying about the dead flowers which are not going to bloom again. You need to understand that a certain number of people come into your life for a certain period of time for a reason and once they walk out your life you need to stop worrying about them and move on. Sometimes you need to lose someone to gain yourself. When people walk out of your life, it's not just they walk out they created an opportunity for someone else to walk in. You may have people who walked out from your life, but focus on people who are still there in your life. It's not the end of life when people who you want to be with you are no longer with you; there is still life until and unless there are people who want you to be part of their life. There is life after love.

Thank You,
My name is Shashank Nandakishor.